Content

Niamh

A Martian comes to stay

It was on the second day of Peter's holiday with his grandmother that the Martian came to the cottage. There was a knock at the door and when he went to open it there was this small green person with webbed feet and eyes on the end of stumpy antennae who said, perfectly politely, "I wonder if I might bother you for the loan of a spanner?"

"Sure," said Peter. "I'll ask my gran."

Gran was in the back garden, it being a nice sunny day. Peter said, "There's a Martian at the door who'd like to borrow a spanner."

Gran looked at him over her knitting. "Is there, dear? Have a look in grandad's toolbox, there should be one there."

That's not what your grandmother would have said? No, nor mine either but Peter's gran was an unusual lady, as you will discover. Grandad had died a few years earlier and she lived alone in this isolated cottage in the country, growing vegetables and keeping chickens, and Peter liked

3

going to stay with her more than almost anything he could think of. Gran was not like most people. She was unflappable and what you might call open-minded, which accounts for everything that happened next.

Peter found the spanner and took it back to the Martian, who held out a rather oddly constructed hand and thanked him warmly. "We've got some trouble with the gears or something and had to make an emergency landing. And now the mechanic says he left his tools back at base. I ask you! It's all a mystery to me – I'm just the steward. Anyway – thanks a lot. I'll bring it back in a minute." And he padded away up the lane. There was no one around, but then there wasn't likely to be: the cottage was a quarter of a mile from the village and hardly anyone came by except the occasional farm tractor and the odd holiday maker who'd got lost. Peter went back into the garden.

"Should have offered him a cup of tea," said Gran. "He'll have had a fair journey, I shouldn't wonder."

"Yes," said Peter. "I didn't think of that."

In precisely three minutes time there was a knock at the door. The Martian was there, looking distinctly agitated. He said, "They've gone."

"Who's gone?" said Peter.

"The others. The spaceship. All of them. They've taken off and left me."

4

Gran, by now, had come through from the garden. She hitched her specs up her nose and looked down at the Martian, who was about three and a half feet high. "You'd best come in," she said, "while we have a think. Gone, you say? Where was it, this thing of yours?"

"Over there," said the Martian, pointing across the lane.

"Ah," said Gran. "Ted Thomas's field."

"The one with the bullocks in," added Peter.

"Bullocks?" said the Martian.

"Big brown animals," explained Peter.

"Animals?" said the Martian.

"Creatures that walk about and eat, like you and me, only different."

The Martian nodded. "I saw them, then. I hoped they were harmless."

"They are," said Peter.

"But curious," said Gran. "They'd have wanted to have a look at this space whatsit, wouldn't they? Stand round it in a circle, making heavy breathing noises. Would they be a bit jumpy, your friends, Mr er...?"

"Very," said the Martian. "We tend to be, when we get off-course. I'm dead jumpy right now. For one thing, I'm frightened of that thing in the corner that makes a ticking noise. Is it going to blow up?"

Peter explained about clocks.

Gran, meanwhile, had put the kettle on. "The way I see it, these friends of Mr, er... looked out and saw Ted's bullocks and lost their heads, and who's to blame them? Still, it's not very nice, leaving him stuck here like this. I mean, it's not as though we can give the village taxi a ring and get him home like that. I don't know what's to be done for the best, I really don't. Meanwhile, we'll have a nice cup of tea."

Tea and a couple of digestive biscuits cheered the Martian up. He sat on the footstool by the stove and apologized for being such a nuisance. "Not at all," said Gran. "We don't get a lot of company round here. It's you I'm bothered about. But anyway, we've got the attic room empty so you're welcome to stop until we can work something out. You'll be company for Peter." She gazed for a moment at the visitor and went on, delicately, "Are you, er, young or old, as you might say?"

"I'm three hundred and twenty-seven," said the Martian.

"Ah," said Gran. "Then there's a bit of an age-gap, on the face of it. Peter's nine. Still, it's the spirit that counts, isn't it? That's what I always find, anyway."

The Martian was an adaptable visitor. He felt the cold rather and preferred to sit right up against the stove and once, with further apologies, got into the oven for a bit to warm up.

"Get a lot of sun, do you, where you come from?" asked Gran. But the Martian was rather vague about his home surroundings; it was different, he said – adding hastily that of course he didn't mean it was better. Once or twice he looked out of the window a trifle nervously. He wanted to know why the trees kept moving.

"It's the wind, dear," said Gran, who tended to take people into the family once she liked them.

"They're not aggressive?"

"Not to speak of."

Later, they watched television. The Martian was interested but inclined to raise questions. "Is it true to life?" he enquired, in the middle of "Top of the Pops".

"No," said Peter. "At least not most people's."

"What about this?" asked the Martian presently, when "Dallas" was on.

"I wouldn't say so," said Gran. "But then I've had a limited experience."

He appreciated "Zoo Quest", which was about South American creatures.

"That's Nature," said Gran. "It's very highly thought of nowadays. Time I got us something to eat." She looked doubtfully at the Martian. "You're not on a special diet or anything like that, I hope?"

But the Martian proved admirably easy to feed. He was a bit wary of sausages but discovered a passion for jam tarts. "You tuck in," said Gran. "You'll be hungry, after that journey."

Over the next couple of days he settled in nicely. He insisted on helping with the washing-up and played Monopoly with Peter. Peter won every time, which he found embarrassing. The Martian didn't seem to grasp the idea of making money. "I'm sorry," he said apologetically. "Why do I want to have more and more of these bits of paper?"

"So that you can buy things," Peter explained.

"Things to eat?"

"Well, no. It's streets and hotels and things, in the game."

"Mind," said Gran, "he's got a point. It's something

I've wondered about myself. Maybe you should try a game of cards."

They played Snap and Rummy but this wasn't much better. The Martian preferred not to win.

"To my mind," said Gran, "they've got a different outlook on life, wherever he comes from." She was knitting the Martian a sweater now. "Would you come here a minute, dear, just so I can measure it across the chest." The Martian stood in front of her obligingly. Gran stretched the knitting across his greenish, rather leathery body. "It's to keep the chill out," she went on. "Being as you feel the cold so. I've no objection at all to a person going around in the altogether if that's what they're used to, let's get that clear. There – that's a nice fit."

The Martian was quite embarrassingly grateful.

He did not venture outside, which seemed on the whole advisable in any case. Neighbours, in remote country districts, tend to be inquisitive about other people's visitors and the Martian would be an odd one to have to explain. "I suppose," said Peter, "we could say he's a distant relative who's come from somewhere abroad."

"That's not going to satisfy some folks I could name,"

said Gran. "Not with him being as unusual-looking as he is. Even if we said he took after another branch of the family. No, it's best if he stays put till his friends come back. D'you think they'll take long, dear?"

The Martian shook his head doubtfully. He said he thought they would come, eventually, but that they might be having difficulty finding the right spot again. "Well, not to worry," said Gran. "We'll just bide our time till they do."

After several days the Martian overcame his worries about trees and various noises that bothered him such as birds and dogs barking, and sat in a deckchair in the garden, wearing Gran's sweater and with a rug round him. On one of these occasions old Mr Briggs from down the lane came past with his dog and stopped for a moment to chat to Gran over the wall. "Ah," he said, glancing over her shoulder. "Got another of your grandchildren stopping with you, then?"

"In a manner of speaking," said Gran evasively.

Mr Briggs departed, calling over his shoulder, "See you at the village fête, Saturday."

Gran sat down again. "It's a shame we can't take him

along to the fête. Be ever so interesting for him. I mean, it's what you want, when you're in foreign parts – have a look at how other people set about things. The Flower Show'll be a treat this year, with the good weather we've been having."

The Martian said wistfully that he'd love to go.

"I wonder," said Gran. "Let's see now. S'pose we…"

And then Peter had a brilliant idea. In the cupboard under the stairs there was an old push-chair that had been used for him and his sister when they were small. If they put the Martian in that and covered him up with a pram-rug and put something round his head, he could pass for a small child. Gran clapped her hands. "Clever boy! There now, we'll have ourselves an outing!" The Martian beamed, if someone with antennae, a mouth somewhat like a letter-box and not much else by way of features can be said to beam.

"You know," Gran confided to Peter later on, when they were alone, "I've really took to him. You can tell he's been brought up nicely, from his manners. There's some human beings I know would be put to shame."

The day of the fête was fine and dry. The Martian was installed in the push-chair, swathed in a blue rug that Gran had crocheted a long time ago and with an old pixie hood that had belonged to Peter's sister on his head. His antennae poked out through two holes, which did not look quite right, so they had to fix a sunshade to the handles of the push-chair and drape some muslin over this; in this way the Martian was only dimly visible as a muffled form. "We'll say he's sensitive to sunstroke," said Gran, "if anyone gets nosy." They set off for the village with Peter in charge of the push-chair.

The Martian was fascinated with everything he saw. He asked them to stop for him to admire the Amoco Garage with its swags of flapping plastic flags and brightly coloured signs about Four Star Petrol and Credit Cards Accepted. He found it, he declared, very beautiful.

"Well," said Gran doubtfully, "to my mind that's on the garish side, but I suppose it's a matter of taste." The Martian said humbly that he probably hadn't been here long enough yet to be much of a judge of these things. He gazed at the display of baked beans tins and cornflakes packets in the window of the Minimarket and asked anxiously if that would be considered handsome. "Not really," said Peter. "I mean, it's the sort of thing that's so ordinary you don't really notice."

"He's seeing a different angle to us," said Gran. "Stands to reason, when you think about it."

The smell of petrol made him sneeze. Mrs Lilly from the Post Office, who happened to be passing at the time, craned her head round to stare into the push-chair. "Bless its little heart, then! Tishoo!" She bent down. "Little boy or a little girl, is it?"

"Boy," said Gran. "I wouldn't be surprised if that cold wasn't giving way to something worse," she added loudly. Mrs Lilly backed away.

They reached the village green, on which the fête was taking place. The band was already playing. The Martian peered out from under the sunshade. "Watch it!" said Peter warningly. "People'll see you." The Martian apologized. "It's just that it's all so exciting."

"We always put on a good show," said Gran modestly. "It's a question of upstaging Great Snoggington down the road, up to a point," she explained. The Martian, under the sunshade, nodded. Gran pointed out the Vicar and the head teacher from the village school and Mr Soper who ran the pub.

"They are your leaders?" asked the Martian.

"In a manner of speaking," said Gran.

They toured the Bring and Buy stall and the Flower Tent. Gran paused to cast a professional eye over the sweet peas. Peter took out his money to see if he had enough left for another ice-cream. Neither of them saw Susie Stubbs, who was aged three and in Peter's opinion the most appalling brat in the village, sidle up to the push-chair. She put out a fat finger and poked the Martian, who sat perfectly still. Susie stuck her face under the sunshade.

There was an earsplitting shriek. Susie's mum, busy in the middle of a piece of juicy gossip with a friend, broke off and came rushing over.

"Ooooh...!" wailed Susie. "An 'orrible fing! An 'orrible fing like a snail! Oooh – I don't like it! Want to go home! Want my mum! Take it away! Ooh, an 'orrible fing in that pram!"

"There, my pet," cooed Susie's mum. "There, there... Did she have a nasty fright, then? Let's buy her an iced lolly, shall we?"

" 'Orrible fing..." howled Susie, pointing at the push-chair.

Gran glared. She jerked the push-chair away, nearly dislodging the Martian.

"There now, my duckie," said Susie's mum. "Why don't you ask the little girl if she'd like to come and play, then."

"Boy," snapped Gran. "Pity he's got such a shocking case of chicken-pox or he'd have liked to, wouldn't you then, Johnnie? 'Bye now, Mrs Stubbs."

An interested group of observers had gathered. Peter and Gran departed hastily. "Sorry about that," said Gran to the Martian. The Martian replied politely that where he came from also young people were sometimes inclined to be tiresome.

They left the Flower Tent, pausing for Gran to have a word with one or two friends. Curiosity, though, had now been aroused; people kept casting interested glances at the push-chair. "That your Ron's youngest?" enquired Mrs Binns from the shop. "Eh?" said Gran loudly; she was expert at producing sudden onsets of deafness when convenient.

Outside, they sat down to watch the police dog display. One of the dogs, which was supposed to be tracking a man who was supposed to be an escaped criminal, kept rushing over and sniffing at the push-chair. "Get away, you brute," snarled Gran. The Martian, beneath the sunshade, kept bravely silent but had turned quite pale when Peter took a look at him. He fetched some orange juice from the Refreshment Tent. "Thank you," said the Martian faintly.

A stout figure swathed in several Indian bedspreads sat under a sign which declared her to be MADAME RITA, THE INTERNATIONALLY FAMOUS PALMIST AND FORTUNE TELLER. "That's the Vicar's wife," said Gran. "I'm not having her nosing around my future." Nevertheless, she veered in that direction. The Vicar's wife, her face blotted out by an enormous pair of sunglasses, seized Gran's hand and predicted a tall dark stranger next Thursday.

"That'll be him that comes to read the meter," said Gran. "Well-built, I'd call him, rather than tall, but never mind."

The Vicar's wife, bending down, lifted the muslin draped over the Martian's sunshade. "What about the baby, then – let's have your hand, duckie." She gave a gasp of horror. "Oh, my goodness, the poor little dear, whatever..."

"Whatever what?" said Gran frostily.

The Vicar's wife dropped the muslin. "Well, he's a nice little thing, of course, but... well... unusual."

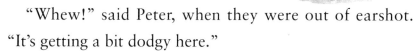

Gran gave her a withering look. "I'd say those specs you've got on aren't doing you any good, Mrs Mervyn. Fashionable they may be but not what I'd call serviceable. Well, I'd best be getting on."

"Whew!" said Peter, when they were out of earshot. "It's getting a bit dodgy here."

Gran agreed. "Anyway, he's seen a bit of our way of life, that's the main thing. We'll get home now."

But the damage had been done. There was gossip. The village had been alerted. The next day, three people turned up at the cottage declaring that they happened to be passing and hadn't seen Gran for a month of Sundays and had been wondering how she was. Gran managed to get rid of them all. The Martian sat by the stove saying sadly that he was afraid he was becoming a problem. "It's not you that's the problem," said Gran. "It's human nature."

All the same, they realized that he could not stay there for ever. "At least not without us becoming world famous," said Peter. "And him being put on the telly and that kind of thing."

"I shouldn't care for that," said the Martian in alarm. "I'm basically very shy."

They discussed what was to be done. The Martian said he thought that probably his companions would be trying to find the spot at which they had landed but were having navigational problems.

"Anything you can think of we could do to lend a hand?" enquired Gran.

"We could signal," said Peter. "In their language. He could tell us what to say."

The Martian became quite excited. He'd need some kind of radio transmitter, he said.

Gran shook her head. "I've not got one of those to hand. But there's Jim's big torch up in the attic. We could flash that, like, when it's dark."

They had their first signal session that evening. The Martian dictated a series of long and short flashes and Peter and Gran took it in turns to stand at the window with the lights off, waving the torch at the sky. Gran thoroughly enjoyed it. She wanted to put in all sorts of extras like invitations to tea and enquiries about whether they preferred fruit cake or a nice jam sponge. She hoped there wouldn't be misunderstandings. "We don't want one of them satellites coming down in Ted Thomas's field. Or a bunch of them R.A.F. blokes."

But nothing happened. They decided to try again the

next night.

They had been at it for an hour or two – with a break to watch "Coronation Street", to which the Martian was becoming dangerously addicted – when there was a knock at the door.

"Oh, it's you, Bert," said Gran. "What's up, then? Don't you start telling me I've got no telly licence, because I have. Top drawer of the dresser, have a look for yourself."

The village policeman was standing there. He said heavily, "I'm obliged to ask you if I might come in and look round the premises, Mrs Tranter."

"What's all this posh talk for?" said Gran. "Come on in. Help yourself." She put the torch on the table.

The policeman eyed it. "Would you mind telling me what you've been employing that for the use of, Mrs Tranter?"

"That," snapped Gran, "is a torch, and if you don't know what torches are for, Bert Davies, then you'll never make sergeant, frankly."

The policeman, a little red now around the neck, met Gran's glare valiantly, eyeball to eyeball. "Would you by any chance, Mrs Tranter, have been passing information to a foreign power?"

There was an awful silence. Peter and the Martian, who was cowering behind the stove, exchanged nervous glances.

"Bert Davies," said Gran at last, "I've known you since you was in nappies. You come here asking that kind of thing once more – just once more – and I'm off down the village to have a word with your mum." She glared at the policeman, who was now a rich strawberry colour to the roots of his hair, and was backing towards the door.

"There's been reports," he said, "reports about flashing lights and that. It's my duty to investigate."

"It's your duty to get back to the village and see about them motor-bike boys that's always charging through over the speed limit," snapped Gran.

It was at that moment that Peter heard a curious

whirring noise from somewhere outside. The policeman, mercifully, was too unnerved to pay any attention, if indeed he had heard anything; he retreated to his car, with as much dignity as he could manage, and drove off into the night…

…At precisely the same time as something brightly spiced with lights loomed above Ted Thomas's field, hovered for a moment, and sank below the line of the hedge.

Peter cried, "They're here!"

"And none before time too," said Gran. The Martian was already on his feet and hurrying to the door. He paused, trying to take off his sweater. "You keep that," said Gran. "Someone might like to copy the pattern, up where you come from."

The Martian held out his hand. "Thank you very much for having me. I've enjoyed it enormously. I wish I could suggest…" He hesitated.

"No, dear," said Gran. "Return visits are out, I'm afraid. Foreign travel doesn't appeal to me nowadays. A week in Llandudno in August does me nicely."

From the field, there was still that whirring noise, and a shimmering orange glow. "Better go," said Peter anxiously, "before anyone comes."

The Martian nodded. He padded out and down the lane. They saw him get smaller and more indistinct and turn in at the gate into the field and then the orange glow got larger and the whirring louder and there was a snap of bright lights and a rush and then silence and darkness.

Gran closed the door. "That, I take it," she said, "was one of them flying saucers. Pity we couldn't have taken a picture. It would have been nice for my album. Put the torch back in the attic, would you, dear. And put that spanner back in your grandad's toolbox, while you're at it. Good thing we had that by us, or we'd never have been able to lend a hand in the first place. I should have made him up some sandwiches for the journey, you know."

And she settled down by the stove with her knitting.

The phantom tollbooth

Milo takes a journey through a strange land, accompanied by a Humbug (who never speaks the honest truth) and Tock, a Watchdog (who worries about people wasting time). They meet Alec Bings, who can see through things, behind and around things, but can't see whatever is under his nose.

Alec raced ahead, laughing and shouting, but soon encountered serious difficulties; for, while he could always see the tree behind the next one, he could never see the next one itself and was continually crashing into it. After several minutes of wildly dashing about, they all stopped for a breath of air.

"I think we're lost," panted the Humbug, collapsing into a large bramble bush.

"Nonsense!" shouted Alec from the high branch on which he sat.

"Do you know where we are?" asked Milo.

"Certainly," he replied, "we're right here on this very spot. Besides, being lost is never a matter of not knowing where you are; it's a matter of not knowing where you aren't – and I don't care at all about where I'm not."

This was much too complicated for the bug to work

out, and Milo had just begun repeating it to himself when Alec said, "If you don't believe me, ask the giant," and he pointed to a small house tucked neatly between two of the largest trees.

Milo and Tock walked up to the door, whose brass name-plate read simply THE GIANT, and knocked.

"Good afternoon," said the perfectly ordinary-sized man who answered the door.

"Are you the giant?" asked Tock doubtfully.

"To be sure," he replied proudly. "I'm the smallest giant in the world. What can I do for you?"

"Are we lost?" said Milo.

"That's a difficult question," said the giant. "Why don't you go round to the back and ask the midget?" And he closed the door.

They walked to the rear of the house, which looked exactly like the front, and knocked at the door, whose name-plate read THE MIDGET.

"How are you?" inquired the man, who looked exactly like the giant.

"Are you the midget?" asked Tock, again with a hint of uncertainty in his voice.

"Unquestionably," he answered. "I'm the tallest Midget in the world. May I help you?"

"Do you think we're lost?" repeated Milo.

"That's a very complicated problem," he said. "Why don't you go round to the side and ask the fat man?" And he, too, quickly disappeared.

The side of the house looked very like the front and back, and the door flew open the very instant they knocked.

"How nice of you to come by," exclaimed the man, who could have been the midget's twin brother.

"You must be the fat man," said Tock, learning not to count too much on appearance.

"The thinnest one in the world,"

he replied brightly: "but if you have any questions, I suggest you try the thin man, on the other side of the house."

Just as they suspected, the other side of the house looked the same as the front, the back, and the side, and the door was again answered by a man who looked precisely like the other three.

"What a pleasant surprise!" he cried happily. "I haven't had a visitor for as long as I can remember."

"How long is that?" asked Milo.

"I'm sure I don't know," he replied. "Now pardon me; I have to answer the door."

"But you just did," said Tock.

"Oh yes, I'd forgotten."

"Are you the fattest thin man in the world?" asked Tock.

"Do you know one that's fatter?" he asked impatiently.

"I think you're all the same man," said Milo emphatically.

The Thin Man

"S-S-S-S-S-H-H-H-H-H-H-H," he cautioned, putting his finger up to his lips and drawing Milo closer. "Do you want to ruin everything? You see, to tall men I'm a midget, and to short men I'm a giant; to the skinny ones I'm a fat man, and to the fat ones I'm a thin man. That way I can hold four jobs at once. As you can see, though,

I'm neither tall nor short nor fat nor thin. In fact, I'm quite ordinary, but there are so many ordinary men that no one asks their opinion about anything. Now what is your question?"

"Are we lost?" asked Milo once again.

"H-h-m-m-m," said the man, scratching his head. "I haven't had such a difficult question for as long as I can remember. Would you mind repeating it? It's slipped my mind."

Milo asked the question for the fifth time.

"My, my," the man mumbled. "I know one thing for certain; it's much harder to tell whether you are lost than whether you were lost, for, on many occasions, where you're going is exactly where you are. On the other hand, you often find that where you've been is not at all where you should have gone, and, since it's much more difficult to find your way back from somewhere you've never left, I suggest you go there immediately and then decide. If you have any more questions, please ask the giant." And he slammed his door and pulled down the blind.

Hello 21st century

34 Saturn Way

Glexbase 8

M. Station h746

GM8 74H

12 October 2092

Dear Samantha,

I am writing to you via a new invention. It enables us to send letters through time.

What is it like in the 20th century? I have been doing a project on it, at school. It must be really hard work! Imagine having to cook your own food!!

Do you have to write on paper at school? We have a computer each at school, that we carry round to all our lessons. It is quite small, and we just use different micro disks for each lesson (that's a type of computer disk).

We don't have to cook our food. We have an Autocuisine. We just type in the food we want, and it comes out, cooked and ready to eat!! We don't have to go shopping for food, either, we just send our order, via computer, and it gets delivered. You can buy almost anything by computer now, but if you want you can go to the shop to buy things too.

We don't have telephones any more, we can contact people by our computers, or use our phone vision. This is like a telephone, but with a camera attached, so you can see the person you're talking to. For entertainment, we have video, computer or hologram games, there is also a new game just come out, where you sit in a chair, put a headset on and it is like a simulator ride! Don't worry, we still have the classics, like Nintendo, Sega and Virtuality. We also have a 3D Holo-tele, where the action is projected into your room as a hologram.

There were lots of wars in the 20th century, weren't there? We haven't had any wars, or aggressions of any kind, for fifty-two years now, which is just as well, as we now have enough weapons to blow up the entire universe!

I had better stop writing now, as there is a limited weight on this Letter-Through-Time scheme. Please write back, it would be so interesting to hear from you.

Best wishes,

Lisa Black

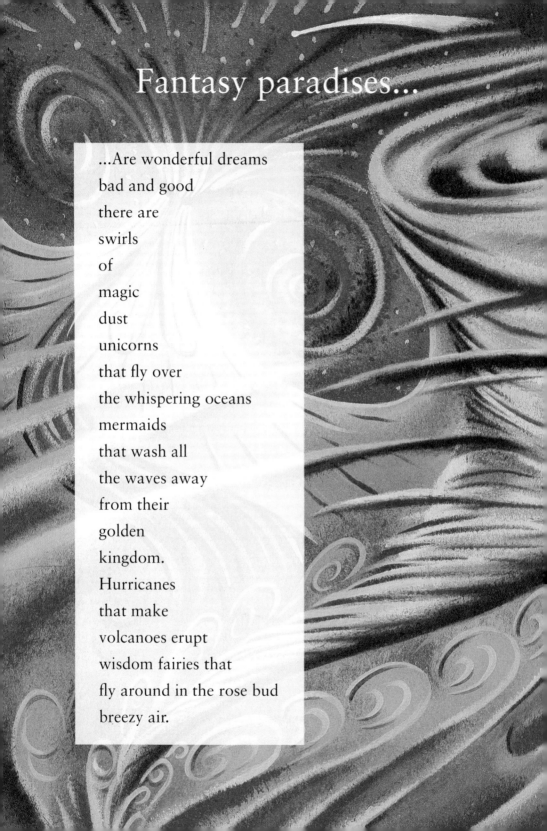

Fantasy paradises...

...Are wonderful dreams
bad and good
there are
swirls
of
magic
dust
unicorns
that fly over
the whispering oceans
mermaids
that wash all
the waves away
from their
golden
kingdom.
Hurricanes
that make
volcanoes erupt
wisdom fairies that
fly around in the rose bud
breezy air.

Satin white mountains
that have
golden
cornfields behind
them.
Fires
that are
whizzed away
by the
flying horses.
Silver
waterfalls
that fall
with
powerful
strength
hands grabbing
for the
dreams.

Emma-Jane Melton

Krindlekrax

"Oh, I know what you think," Corky said, dunking the biscuit in his tea and starting to lick the chocolate. "You think I've always been a caretaker and I've always worn a white overall and had grey hair and walked with a walking stick. But that's not true. Ten years ago, my hair was black and I walked without a limp, and I didn't work at St George's School."

"So where did you work?" Ruskin asked, sipping his tea.

"In the sewers," Corky replied.

"The sewers!" Ruskin exclaimed, nearly dropping his cup.

"Yes, my dear boy. The sewers. Underground where all the dirty water is. In the smelly dark. At least, that's how most people think of it. But I never thought of it like that. For me it was beautiful. The walls are bright green and the water makes a gentle, trickling noise. There are chambers big as cathedrals, and waterfalls so high you

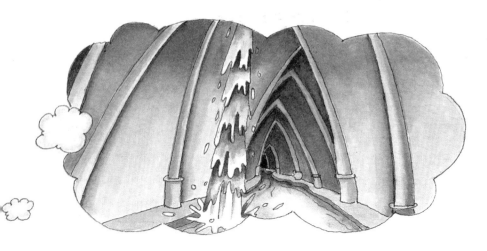

can't see the top. And when you speak, your voice echoes round you a million times until your ears ring and you get giddy. It's another world down there and I loved everything about it. I felt like an explorer. Being down there was a true adventure for me, my dear boy."

"If it was dark," Ruskin said, "how did you see?"

"I'll show you," Corky replied.

Corky got up and went over to a wardrobe. He opened the door, removed something wrapped in newspaper, then returned to the table.

"What's that?" Ruskin asked.

"Open it and see," Corky said, handing it to him. The newspaper was very old and had turned yellow. It smelled of damp and dust.

Carefully, Ruskin peeled away the paper, like peeling an onion, and inside he found a tin helmet with a torch stuck on the front.

"I wonder if it still works," Corky said. And he reached over and flicked a switch on top of the torch.

The torch lit up.

Corky took the helmet from Ruskin and put it on.

The torch gleamed like a brilliant third eye.

"How do I look?" Corky asked.

"Wonderful," Ruskin said.

"That's how I looked in those days," Corky said, sighing. "I was younger and I was wonderful and I felt like an explorer in the underground world of green cathedrals and majestic waterfalls."

"So why did you leave?" Ruskin asked. "Why did you stop being an explorer and become a caretaker?"

"Because," Corky replied, "I was the one who found Krindlekrax."

Ruskin shivered so violently he nearly dropped his cup.

"Are you cold, my dear boy?" asked Corky.

"No. I just..."

"More tea?" asked Corky.

"No," Ruskin said.

"Are you ill?"

"Just finish your story!" cried Ruskin, in the closest his squeaky whisper of a voice could get to a shout. "Tell me about Krindlekrax!"

Corky took a deep breath.

"One day," Corky said, "I was underground when I heard a noise. A noise like I'd never heard before. A sort of crying sound. 'Eeeek' went the noise. I looked all round. My torch beam cut through the darkness. And there... there – on a ledge beside the trickling water – I saw something move. It was about the size of a shoe and bright green and had tiny sharp teeth. It was eating a slice of toast."

"What was it?" Ruskin asked, staring at Corky and clutching the edge of his seat.

"A baby crocodile, my dear boy," Corky replied.

"But how did it get there?"

"I never found that out. But there it was. Bright green and munching toast. There was marmalade on the toast and orange rind was stuck between the crocodile's teeth. There was something enticing about the tiny creature. I wanted to touch it. So I stepped forward. My feet went splash in the water and the light from my torch shone in the animal's eyes, making them bright red."

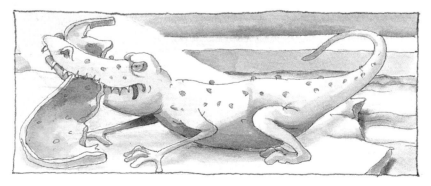

"Were you scared?" Ruskin asked.

"No, my dear boy. I just wanted to get closer to the crocodile, to feel its skin." Corky licked a chocolate biscuit for a while, then continued, "Slowly, I reached out... I could feel the crocodile's warm breath on my fingertips. And then, suddenly, the crocodile snapped its jaws shut. I managed to get my finger out of the way just in time. 'Clack!' went the jaws. Like two bits of metal clanging together. I took a step back, slipped and fell into the water. The water went up my nose and into my ears and made me cough and splutter. But I didn't have time to cough and splutter for long."

"Why, Corky?" Ruskin asked.

"Because the crocodile was already chasing after me," Corky replied. "I ran down the tunnel. The crocodile was very fast. I could hear its cracking jaws and the swish of its tail. I ran through the dirty water, hardly looking where I was going. I started to panic. For a moment I thought I was lost and would never find the ladder that led up to the surface again. 'Help!' I called. 'Help me, someone.'

"My voice echoed all round me. But no help came. No one could hear me. I was underground, my dear boy, and no living thing could hear me. Except..."

"The crocodile!" Ruskin interrupted.

"Exactly," Corky said. "Except the crocodile. But – suddenly – I saw the ladder. I grabbed it and started to climb. I was half-way up when I felt a terrible pain in my knee." Corky touched his leg, the one with the limp. "I looked down and saw the crocodile biting my knee. I shook my leg frantically. But the crocodile wouldn't let go. Its tiny jaws were clenched tight. Deeper and deeper its teeth went into my skin. I was yelling out. Finally, I hit the crocodile as hard as I could. It let go and fell back into the watery darkness. I heard it go splash."

Corky poured himself another cup of tea.

"Thirsty work," Corky remarked, "all this storytelling."

"So that's how you got your limp," Ruskin said.

"Exactly, my dear boy," Corky said. "I went to hospital and a doctor put a bandage round my knee and told me I'd be all right. But I wasn't! The crocodile had bitten through a tendon or something and I had to use a walking stick." Corky picked up the packet of biscuits and looked inside. "Only one left," he said. "Do you want it, my dear boy?"

"No, you can have it," Ruskin replied.

"You sure? I wouldn't want to cheat you of your share of the delicious chocolate."

"I'm sure, Corky. Just tell me the rest of the story. Is that why you left your job underground and became a caretaker instead?"

"Almost," Corky replied, licking the biscuit, "but not quite. I stopped going underground, but I still worked for the same firm. They gave me a job in an office instead. I stayed there for a couple of years. And then, one day, a worker went sick and they needed someone to go underground in his place to check a few leaks and rusty pipes."

"And you were the one that went," Ruskin said.

"That's right," Corky said, his tongue covered with chocolate. "I put my helmet on – this very helmet, with its torch – and went down into the darkness again."

"And… and you saw the crocodile again?" suggested Ruskin.

"Oh, not at first," Corky said. "At first I didn't even think about it. I just concentrated on walking through the water without slipping over. And then… and then I heard it."

"What?"

"A roar. A roar like I'd never heard before. Like a million car tyres screeching all at once. It made my bones shake."

"Were you scared?" Ruskin asked.

"Very."

"Because you knew what it was?"

"That's right, my dear boy," Corky said, licking the last of the chocolate from the biscuit and throwing it away. "I knew that for two years the baby crocodile had been drinking the dirty water and eating the remains of food. I knew that it had been growing and growing. And I knew something else. I knew that biting my knee had given it a taste for my blood. I knew that it had been growing and waiting for me to return so it could finish me off once and for all."

Ruskin leant forward and squeezed Corky's hand.

"What did you do?" Ruskin asked, eyes wide.

"Well, I didn't panic, my dear boy," Corky replied. "That's the worst thing to do. Never panic. So... slowly and calmly... I turned round and limped towards the ladder. I tried to be as quiet as possible. The splashing of my feet in the water sounded so loud to me. And then... then I heard it again. That terrible roar. I knew the crocodile was getting closer."

"Although it wasn't just a crocodile any more, was it, Corky?" Ruskin said. "It had got another name."

"It was Krindlekrax," Corky said. "I just knew that was its name. The roar of Krindlekrax filled my ears. I saw the ladder and reached out. I could hear splashing coming towards me. I knew Krindlekrax was getting closer and closer. I ran up the ladder. And, in those last few moments, I glanced down to see what was chasing after me."

"What did it look like?" Ruskin asked.

"Huge and dark," Corky replied, "with pointed claws and sharp teeth and breath as hot as fire. It was the most terrible thing I had ever seen." Corky leaned back and took his helmet off. "When I got home that evening," he said, "I saw that all my hair had turned white. The sight of Krindlekrax had drained the colour from me."

Feed the plants

My mum said "Feed the plants"
And went. I did them all. No thanks
From her or them. Now she's banging on the door.
"Open up!" I shout back from the floor
"I can't! The busy Lizzie's leaning on it.
I think she's just about to vomit.
She says she's feeling dizzy. Honest."

Mum's shouting now. She can't see in.
The windows are all cabbage-green.
"It's no good shouting," I shout back.
"The spider plant's got me round the neck
I'm kind of tied up for a bit
I don't know what I've done to it.
I think you ought to know," I gasp
As it tightens up its friendly clasp
"They liked the bread and marmalade
And finished off the buns you made
The fried fish and tomato sauce
Oh, and the apple pie, of course.
And then I gave them cold rice pud
I don't think it's done them any good.
I tried to make a pot of tea
But this spider plant grabbed hold of me.
It's got me in a kind of lock – it
Seems to be puking in my pocket."

"You fool," Mum shouts, still banging and thudding
"What a terrible waste of good rice pudding."

Berlie Doherty

Space oddities

The universe is full of strange things, "oddities" and unexpected facts. Let me begin with a trick question: how far can you see without a telescope?

I suppose most people would say, "Well, a few miles." The true answer is very different. On a dark night during autumn look up at the constellation or star group we call Andromeda. It is not hard to identify – any outline star-map will show you where it is. In Andromeda you may be able to make out a tiny patch of what looks like a luminous haze. I agree that it is not at all conspicuous but binoculars will show it well. This is the Great Galaxy in Andromeda, a huge star system so far away that its light, travelling at 300,000 kilometres every second, takes over two million years to reach us.

If you work it out you will find the distance of the Andromeda Galaxy is about 21,000,000,000,000,000,000 kilometres. This is the greatest distance that you can see with your unaided eyes!

Coming back to our own part of the universe – the Sun's family, or Solar System – where would you find a planet where the atmosphere presses down about a hundred times as strongly as it does on you at the present moment, and

where the temperature is not far short of 480 degrees Celsius? The answer is Venus, which is a world about the same size as the Earth, but in a completely different state. Moreover, the dense atmosphere on Venus is made up chiefly of the gas we call carbon dioxide, which we could not breathe (carbon dioxide is the gas which makes drinks fizzy). An astronaut who went to Venus and stepped unprotected out of the spaceship would at once be fried, poisoned and squashed. It does not sound a very pleasant sort of place – yet if you look at Venus with the naked eye, it looks misleadingly cool and inviting.

Another oddity, of a different kind, is the minor planet Eros, which can pass within about 23,000,000 kilometres of us. Eros has no atmosphere and is shaped rather like a sausage.

If Eros is like a sausage, then Phobos, the larger of the two dwarf moons of Mars, is more like a potato!

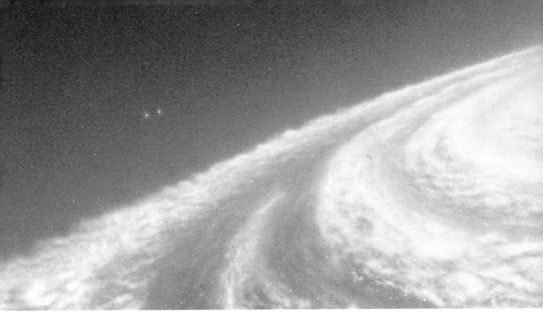

The space probe Mariner 9 (1971–2) and the Russian Phobos space probe (1990s) photographed it at close range and it turned out to be anything but a perfect globe. It has a very weak pull; if you happened to go there and throw a cricket ball upward, the ball would never come back because Phobos' feeble gravity would be unable to hold it.

Far away, well beyond our Solar System, we have stars of all kinds. Take Castor, in the constellation of the Twins; it looks like a single star but we know that it is not. A telescope shows that it is made up of two stars, so close together that with the naked eye they appear as one. Using less direct methods, we can show that each of the two is again double; and another much fainter double star is associated with the system. So Castor is a sort of "family party" made up of six suns, four brilliant and two red and dim. Other multiple stars of this kind are known and

Artist's impression of our galaxy, the Milky Way, as it might be seen from a spacecraft.

double stars are surprisingly common.

Then we have very old stars, the strange white dwarfs, which are so dense that a cupful of their material would weigh many tonnes; one of these is the faint companion of Sirius, the brightest star in the sky. (Look for it in winter, in line with Orion's belt.)

There is another oddity in the constellation of Taurus, the Bull, though you will not be able to see it unless you use a telescope or very strong binoculars. It is known as the Crab Nebula, and it is a mass of gas; we know that it is all that is left of a star which blew itself to pieces, and was seen by Chinese astronomers in the year 1054. Deep inside it is a very small, super-dense body which we call a "pulsar", and which is so dense that you could pack a thousand million tonnes of it into a matchbox!

The space patrol problem

The crippled alien space-craft was in orbit around the plant Xzyg. Fred Fortitude's Earth Federation Space Cruiser was in an identical orbit about 160 kilometres behind the alien ship.

How could Fred close the gap? He had six thruster rockets to choose from. One would fire towards the planet's surface, and one away. A third would fire to the left and a fourth to the right. The fifth was positioned so that it would fire towards the alien ship and the sixth away from it. Which would be the best one to use?

Solution on inside back cover

That stormy night

That stormy night
when the wind moaned like a wolf
and bent the trees, and shook the house
I wondered if it could blow the stars away.

What then – if their glittering dust
lay among the fallen leaves next day
crystals and splinters in the morning light?
I'd sweep them up and put them in a box

and bring them home to you. You'd say
Nonsense. What you see up there
is light that's millions of years away
you know that, don't you?

Yes. I know. But still
I'd shake my box of stardust
hold it tight
knowing the wind had blown the stars away

that stormy night.

Berlie Doherty

Shed in space

My Grandad Lewis
On my mother's side,
Had two ambitions.
One was to take first prize
For shallots at the village show,
And the second
Was to be a space commander.
Every Tuesday
After I'd got their messages,
He'd lead me with a wink
To his garden shed
And there, amongst the linseed

And the sacks of peat and horse manure
He'd light his pipe
And settle in his deck chair.
His old eyes on the blue and distant
That no one else could see,
He'd ask,
"Are we A O.K. for lift off?"
Gripping the handles of the lawn mower
I'd reply:
"A O.K."
And then

Facing the workbench,
In front of shelves of paint and creosote
And racks of glistening chisels,
He'd talk to Mission Control.
"Five–Four–Three–Two–One–Zero–
We have lift off.
This is Grandad Lewis talking,
Do you read me?
Britain's first space shed
Is rising majestically into orbit
From its launch pad
In the allotments
In Lakey Lane."
And so we'd fly,
Through timeless afternoons
'Till tea time came,
Amongst the planets
And mysterious suns,
While the world
Receded like a dream:
Grandad never won
That prize for shallots,
But as the captain
Of an intergalactic shed
There was no one to touch him.

Gareth Owen

Crash landing

Charity leaned back on her pillow. Three pages left. She'd have time to finish her book and find out what happened to the Demon Headmaster before Dad got in from his evening walk round the farmyard.

As she flipped the last page, there was a noise overhead, low in the sky. An engine coughed, stuttered. Louder – very loud – something scraped the roof, clanged in the gutter and swooshed past her window, huge and dark.

Then the light went out.

For a second it felt like the end of the world. Then the pigs began to squeal, chickens squawked, goats bleated and the bull bellowed from his field beyond the sheep pasture.

Charity pushed her feet into her old trainers, threw the book down and leaped downstairs. Mum and Dad were outside with a big flashlight.

"Hey, wait!" Charity called across the yard.

Beyond them, in the light, she could see a tangled mess of telephone wires and electric cables twisted into the rotor of a helicopter. Below, jagged and glinting in the torchlight, was the broken glass bubble with a tall figure stiff and upright inside.

As she shouted, Dad turned, and shone the light into her eyes, blinding her to everything else.

"Get inside, Charity!"

"But I want to help!"

"Fetch Tom then," shouted Mum. "He'll have to take the van and go to the phone-box."

"But I don't –" Charity started. Then realized that she

didn't need details. They wanted everything. Fire, police and ambulance.

She raced along the footpath to Tom's cottage, sure-footed even in the dark. Past the broken gate that was held together with a loop of string, over the poached mud in the cow pasture, through the hole in the hedge where sheep escaped. Calling all the time.

"Tom! There's been an accident! The phone's dead. Tom!"

Suddenly he was there, appearing quietly as he always did, with his old cap pulled forward on his bald head. "I'll take the van then. Never fear!"

That was all. No fuss. No questions. He put his arm round Charity's shoulder and they walked back. As they passed the tumbled down pigsty and came into the farmyard, Charity looked across at the helicopter. The tall, upright figure was still in the cockpit. Something about it made her shudder. Tom patted her arm.

"Off to bed now. No place for you."

Charity stopped at the kitchen door and heard peace return as Tom walked into the farmyard. Squeals and squawks died away, replaced by occasional sleepy snuffles and clucks. And the sound of people talking.

54

It's all right, Charity thought, climbing the stairs. Now Tom's come. He'll keep it all all right.

The next thing she knew was waking up with the sunlight hot across her face and the sound of Alice, her pet lamb, baaing at the kitchen door. She sat up and looked at her watch.

Eleven o'clock? Jumping up, she pulled on her clothes and scurried down to the kitchen, calling out as she went. "Why didn't you wake me up?"

Her mother was standing at the kitchen table, spreading a neat little lacy cloth on the best black tray. "Sssh!"

"What?" Charity stopped at the bottom of the stairs.

"I said hush, Charity. You'll disturb the Visitor."

"The who?"

Mother pointed up at the spare room over their heads. "Ssh! He says he can't be moved until his leg's mended. He was just lucky the helicopter didn't catch fire."

"Oh," Charity remembered the sinister upright figure in the broken bubble. "We're looking after the pilot?"

She said it quite casually, but the effect was extraordinary. Her mother stopped laying the tray. She stood up very straight, her face went blank and she spoke in a brisk, mechanical voice.

"It is a privilege to have the Visitor and a pleasure to look after him."

"What?" said Charity.

Her mother repeated exactly the same words in exactly the same voice. "It is a privilege to have the Visitor and a pleasure to look after him."

A long shiver went up Charity's back, and inside her head a small voice whispered, Something's wrong. But what?

She turned away to open the back door. The moment the crack was wide enough, Alice was through, butting her curly head against Charity's legs and baaing with pleasure.

Above their heads, the brass handbell rang loudly. Charity's mother looked nervously upwards and then picked up the neatly laid coffee tray.

"I'll take that," Charity said, but her mother didn't even hear her. She carried the tray upstairs herself and a few seconds later Charity heard the low mutter of voices above.

"I don't like this," she whispered to Alice. "I don't like it one little bit."

But before she could work out why, the car drove into the yard. Her father stepped out, shutting the door quietly instead of slamming it as usual, and came in carrying a bundle of leaflets.

"Hallo, Charity. Sleep well?"

Charity nodded. "Been into town?"

"Had to ask them to fix the wires. And I wanted to pick up a few things. Any coffee?"

Charity put the kettle on. Then, idly, she looked at the leaflets. Capital letters shouted slogans at her:

THE GOAT PRODUCTION LINE – FROM UDDER TO CHEESE IN ONE BUILDING!!!!

COOPER'S CATTLE CONCENTRATES – IMPROVE MILK YIELD BY 15%!!!

Turn your chickens into egg machines!!!!

CIVILIZED PIGS FATTEN UP IN PIG-TECH PARLOURS

At first she thought it was a joke. But she read a page or two and looked up, horrified. "Dad! Why have you got these?"

Her father looked out of the window at the untidy, tumbled down farmyard. "We're very inefficient. We'd make more money if the farm was – well, more like a factory."

"But you've always said you'd never do anything like that!" Charity shouted, and Alice baaed as if she agreed.

Her father looked vague. "Yes, I have, haven't I."

Charity shivered again. "He's made you do it, hasn't he? The Visitor."

Horrifyingly, her father's face went blank, as her mother's had done and the same mechanical words came out of his mouth. "It is a privilege to have the Visitor and a pleasure to look after him!"

"No!" whispered Charity. "No!"

At that moment, her mother came down the stairs. Pointing a finger at Alice, she chanted, "Animals are insanitary and should be kept outside."

It was the last straw. Grabbing Alice, Charity bolted for the only safe place she knew. The top field, where Tom was lifting potatoes.

Alice was really too big to carry and Charity was out of breath when she got there, but Tom waited patiently while she panted everything out.

"– it's horrible," she finished. "I don't know what's happening, but – if you'd heard them and seen those foul leaflets."

Tom took off his cap and scratched his head. Then he stood up. "Reckon I'd best go up and have a word with Farmer. Here." He tossed the keys of the tractor. "Make yourself useful while I'm gone."

Charity had been driving the tractor since she was nine, but she couldn't bear to turn on the engine or do anything else except stare at the track, waiting for Tom to come back.

When he did, she hardly recognized him. He was slumped over, dragging his feet and hanging his head. Charity jumped up and ran to him.

"What's the matter?"

"A week's notice," he said softly.

"What?"

"I'm too old, he says. I've to leave next week – get out of the cottage and all." Tom looked up at Charity. "I wouldn't want to stay, anyway. Not on the sort of farm he's planning."

"It's that Visitor," Charity said bitterly. "He's changed them somehow. As if he's – as if he's hypnotized them."

She looked anxiously at Tom, in case he turned mechanical too, but he just frowned in his usual slow way.

"He's got the eyes for hypnotizing all right. Big sharp green ones."

Inside Charity's head, ideas suddenly began to move. Sharp eyes... a helicopter... people talking as if they'd been hypnotized... everything being made efficient... But it wasn't possible!

Was it?

"We've got to stop him taking over, Tom."

"How?" Tom said gloomily. "Can't scare him off. He's no coward. Didn't even squeak when we were cutting him out of the helicopter. Just asked to borrow a pair of sunglasses. Cool as a cucumber."

Sunglasses! Suddenly Charity had a brilliant, terrifying idea. "Tom." She clutched his arm. "Have you still got your sunglasses? The ones your daughter sent you?"

"Those mirror specs? Maybe."

He would have. He never threw anything away. Not even a pair of one-way sunglasses that looked like little mirrors to everyone else. Reflecting their faces back to them. Reflecting their eyes…

If only I dare, Charity thought as they walked down to Tom's cottage.

Half an hour later she stood outside the spare-room door with the mirror specs in her pocket, terrified. But there was no way out. She couldn't let Tom be sent away. With a quick knock, she pushed the door open.

As soon as she saw the tall, thin man sitting up in bed, she knew she was right. His paper-white face was stern behind Dad's sunglasses.

"Yes?" he snapped.

Charity stepped inside. "I want to talk to you."

The Visitor frowned. "Idle talk is inefficient and time-wasting."

"It's not idle. It's important. You can't take over our farm and run it how you want to. It's wrong."

"Your opinion is unimportant."

"Rubbish!" Charity said fiercely. "I'm going to stop you."

The Visitor frowned again. "I thought you wouldn't trouble me, but I must revise my plans." Slowly he took off Dad's sunglasses. His eyes were extraordinary. Large, luminous. Sea-green.

Charity felt the mirror specs in her pocket. Not yet.

The Visitor leaned forward. "I think you are feeling sleepy. You are so sleepy." His voice was soft and crooning.

Charity's fingers curled round the specs. Not yet.

"So very, very tired and sleepy."

Her eyelids were heavy… Beginning to droop…

Now!

She whipped the mirror specs out of her pocket, put them on and closed her eyes. Please let it work! It had to.

"So sleepy," the voice droned on. "Tired and... sleepy... and... can't keep... your eyes..."

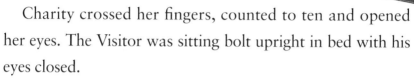

Please!

"So very... very..." The voice died away and stopped.

Charity crossed her fingers, counted to ten and opened her eyes. The Visitor was sitting bolt upright in bed with his eyes closed.

"Hypnotized," whispered Charity. "You've –" He didn't move. "– HYPNOTIZED YOURSELF!" she yelled. He stayed completely still, with his eyes closed.

Taking off the mirror specs, Charity let herself quietly out of the bedroom and walked down to the kitchen.

"Mum – Dad –"

They glanced up from the plans of the new super-efficient Milking Parlour.

"It's the Visitor," Charity said. "I think we should call the doctor. He seems to be – unconscious."

When the ambulance came, she was curled up on her bed making paper darts out of all the factory farm leaflets. She sent one swooping after the ambulance and then picked up *The Prime Minister's Brain* to finish reading about the Demon Headmaster. The last sentence jumped out at her.

I wonder where he came down?

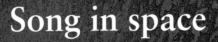

Song in space

When man first flew beyond the sky
He looked back into the world's blue eye.
Man said: What makes your eye so blue?
Earth said: The tears in the ocean do.
Why are the seas so full of tears?
Because I've wept so many thousand years.
Why do you weep as you dance through space?
Because I am the Mother of the Human Race.

Adrian Mitchell

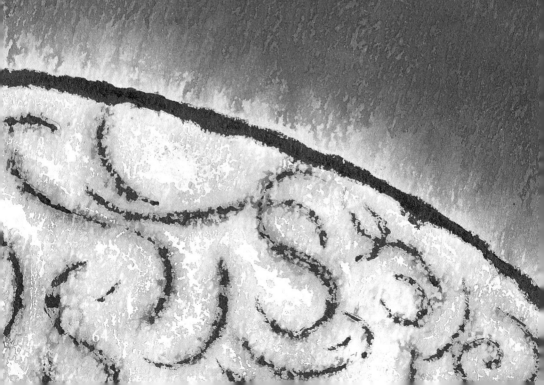